Karen's New Bike

**Look for these
and other books about Karen
in the
Baby-sitters Little Sister series:**

Little Sister

Karen's New Bike
Ann M. Martin

Illustrations by Susan Tang

A
LITTLE APPLE
PAPERBACK

SCHOLASTIC INC.
New York Toronto London Auckland Sydney

*The author gratefully acknowledges
Stephanie Calmenson
for her help
with this book.*

ISBN 0-590-48307-2

12 11 10 9 8 7 6 5 4 3 2 1   5 6 7 8 9/9 0/0

Printed in the U.S.A.   40

First Scholastic printing, June 1995

Surprising
Announcements

Miss Mary, Mack, Mack, Mack
All dressed in black, black, black
With silver buttons, buttons, buttons
All down her back, back, back!

I was on the playground at recess with my friends, Hannie and Nancy. We were singing silly songs as loudly as we could.

Hannie Papadakis and Nancy Dawes are my two best friends. We call ourselves the Three Musketeers.

Who am I? I am Karen Brewer. I am seven years old. I have blonde hair, blue eyes, and a bunch of freckles. Oh, yes. I wear glasses. I even have two pairs. I have a blue pair for reading. I have a pink pair for the rest of the time.

Ringggg! It was time to go back to our second-grade class.

I waved good-bye to Hannie and Nancy when we reached our room. They sit all the way at the back. I sit at the front with the other kids who wear glasses. On one side of me is Ricky Torres. (He is my pretend husband.) On the other side of me is Natalie Springer. For a minute I did not see Natalie. Then she popped up from under the desk. She must have been pulling up her socks. Natalie's socks are always drooping.

"Please settle down, class," said Ms. Colman. "I have an announcement to make."

Oh, goody! I love Ms. Colman's Surprising Announcements.

"What is it?" I called out.

"Karen! You must have forgotten our rules," said Ms. Colman.

"Sorry," I replied. "But I really do remember the rules. I just forget to follow them sometimes."

I recited the rules for Ms. Colman. They are no calling out, and please use your indoor voice.

Ms. Colman smiled at me. She is a very wonderful teacher. Even when I get excited and forget to follow the rules she does not yell or get mad.

"This month is Bike Safety Month," continued Ms. Colman. "Everyone in school will be learning how to ride their bikes safely. We will learn traffic rules. We will learn about the important safety gear we need to wear. And we will learn how to keep a bike in safe working order. But that is not all."

Oh, boy. I wanted to call out again, but I did not. I bounced up and down in my seat instead. Keeping quiet is hard work.

"Our town will also hold a bike-a-thon this month," said Ms. Colman. "We need to raise money for the Stoneybrook Medical Center. I know all of you will work hard to help out."

I turned to Hannie and Nancy and made the thumbs-up sign. Raising money for a good cause is always fun. And the Three Musketeers need to know about bike safety. We ride our bikes all the time.

These were very good Surprising Announcements.

The Bike Parade

"Do you want to come over this afternoon?" I asked Hannie. "We could ride our bikes in honor of Bike Safety Month."

We were walking home from the school bus. This month I was living at my big house. Next month I would live at my little house. (I will tell you about my two houses later.)

"Sure," replied Hannie. "I will get my bike and bring it over. See you soon."

When I walked in the door, Nannie was

waiting for me. Nannie is my stepgrand-mother. I love her.

Emily Michelle was hanging onto Nan-nie's dress. Emily is my little sister. She is two and a half.

"Hi, Karen!" called Andrew. Andrew is my little brother. He is four going on five. He was coming out of the kitchen with a stack of crackers in his hand.

"Why don't you wash up and come to the kitchen, Karen. I have a snack ready for you," said Nannie.

"Okay. But I will have to eat fast. Hannie is coming over," I said.

I dropped my knapsack in my room and washed up. Then I went to the kitchen. I gobbled up some crackers and cheese. I washed my snack down with apple juice.

Ding-dong! The doorbell rang. It was Hannie.

"I will see you later," I said to Nannie. "We are going outside to ride our bikes."

"Please do not ride too far. Wear your

helmets. And be sure to watch for cars in driveways," said Nannie.

"You do not have to worry," I replied. "This is Bike Safety Month. We will be extra, extra careful."

Hannie and I went out to the garage. That is where I keep my bike. It is powder blue with scratches and rust. It is a hand-me-down bike that used to belong to Kristy.

"Hannie, do my tires look flat to you?" I asked.

"I do not think so. Your tires look the same way they always do," replied Hannie. "But one of the spokes on the back wheel is bent."

My bike looked awfully old. I was afraid if I stared at it too long, it would fall apart in front of my eyes. But maybe it looked this way all the time. Maybe I was just noticing it today because of Bike Safety Month.

"Let's ride down the street and see who is around," said Hannie.

I put on my helmet. Then I sat on my bike. As soon as I did, I noticed something else. My bike was too small for me. My knees practically touched the handlebars when I put my feet on the pedals.

Oh, well. It was not the greatest bike. But it still worked. It would get me up and down the street.

Toot toot! I squeezed the horn as I rode down the driveway.

Lots of kids were out riding their bikes. David Michael was riding with Linny. David Michael is my stepbrother. He is seven like me. Linny is Hannie's brother. He is nine years old. We tooted our horns and waved.

Then we saw Melody and Bill Korman. Melody is seven. Bill is nine.

Next Andrew came zooming along the sidewalk on his tricycle.

"I have an idea!" I said. "We can have a bike parade. Everyone who wants to be in it, follow me!"

Toot toot! I rode up the street and everyone followed. I love being the leader. But I know I cannot be the leader all the time. So we turned our bikes around. Then David Michael was the leader. We took turns until everyone had had a chance. We rode up and down and round and round. *Toot toot!*

The bike parade was fun. I decided that Andrew and I should have a bike parade with our friends at the little house sometime. I started thinking about my little-house bike. It was old, too. It came from a second-hand store.

I had two old bikes at two different houses. Do you know what? I have two of lots of things. I will tell you why.

Two Houses, Two Bikes

The reason I have two houses and two bikes is because my parents are divorced.

When I was very little, I lived in one big house in Stoneybrook, Connecticut, with Mommy, Daddy, and Andrew. Then Mommy and Daddy started to fight a lot. They said they loved Andrew and me very much. But they did not love each other anymore. So they decided to get a divorce.

Mommy moved out of the big house with Andrew and me. She moved to a little house not too far away. Then she met a man named Seth. He and Mommy got married. So now Seth is my stepfather. He lives in the little house with Mommy, Andrew, and me. Some pets live with us, too. There is Rocky, Seth's cat; Midgie, Seth's dog; Emily Junior, my pet rat; and Bob, Andrew's hermit crab.

Daddy stayed at the big house. It is the house he grew up in. He met someone new, too. Her name is Elizabeth. She and Daddy got married. So Elizabeth is my stepmother. She lives at the big house with us. She was married before and has four children. They are my stepbrothers and stepsister. I already told you about David Michael. There is also Kristy, who is thirteen and the best stepsister ever, and Sam and Charlie, who are so old they are in high school.

And I told you about my other sister, Emily. But I did not tell you that Daddy and Elizabeth adopted her. She came from a faraway country called Vietnam. Emily is a very good little sister. That is why I named my pet rat after her.

Nannie came to live at the big house after Emily was adopted. She wanted to help take care of her. But really she helps take care of all of us.

Here are the pets who live at the big house: Shannon, David Michael's Bernese mountain dog puppy; Boo-Boo, Daddy's cranky old cat; Crystal Light the Second, my goldfish; Goldfishie, Andrew's you-know-what; and Emily Junior and Bob, who live wherever Andrew and I are living.

I have special names for Andrew and me. I call us Andrew Two-Two and Karen Two-Two. (I got those names from a book Ms. Colman read to our class. It is called *Jacob Two-Two Meets the Hooded Fang.*) I call us two-twos because we have two of so many things. We have two houses and two families, two mommies and two daddies, two cats and two dogs. We have clothes and books at each house. I have my two bikes and Andrew has two tricycles. I have two stuffed cats. Goosie lives at the little house. Moosie lives at the big house. I even have my two best friends. Nancy lives next door to the little house. Hannie lives across the street from the big house.

Now you know why I have two bikes. And since I have two bikes, I guess it is twice as important for me to know the safety rules. I would have to listen carefully to Ms. Colman in school.

A Talk with Daddy

"See you tomorrow at the bus stop!" I called to Hannie.

Our bike parade was over. It was almost time for dinner. Inside the big house, things were a lot busier than before. That was because everyone had come home.

"What's for dinner?" I asked Nannie.

"Pizza and salad," she replied.

Yes! One of my favorites.

The ten of us sat down to eat dinner together. It sounded as though we were all talking at once.

I wanted to talk to Daddy about something special. But I decided it would have to wait.

After dinner Daddy went to the living room. I sat down beside him.

"How was school today?" he asked.

"I had a really good day," I replied. "Ms. Colman made two Surprising Announcements."

"Oh, really? What were they?"

I told him about Bike Safety Week and the bike-a-thon. He thought these were both very good things.

"You know something, Daddy," I said. "My bikes are very old. I am not too sure they are safe. And the bike I have here is too small for me. Maybe that is dangerous, too."

"I have the feeling there is something you would like to ask me," said Daddy, smiling.

"I have the feeling you are right," I replied. "Daddy, can I get a new bike? I know just the kind I want. It is called the Cougar

Cat. I saw one that was hot pink and purple."

"Bikes are very expensive," said Daddy. "But it probably is time to get you a new one."

"Yea!" I cried.

"I will make a deal with you. If you pay for part of the bike, I will pay for the rest," said Daddy.

"Deal," I said. I shook Daddy's hand. Then I gave him a big hug and went up to my room.

"I am going to get a new bike soon!" I told Moosie. "I have to think of a way to make money to help pay for it."

I found some pink paper and a purple marker. I hoped those colors would inspire me.

My friends and I have had to earn money before. We have been car washers, gardeners, baby-sitters, and lemonade vendors. What else could I do? I looked at my blank piece of paper. And guess what. The blank page gave me a gigundoly good idea.

"I will make stationery and sell it," I told Moosie. "Everyone likes to have personal stationery. Whoever orders some from me will have their name at the top. I will make a beautiful drawing at the bottom. Isn't that a good idea?"

I could hardly wait to get started. I had lots of colored paper and markers. That was all I needed.

I decided to begin taking orders right away.

Stationery for Sale

The first thing I did was make up a flier.

I drew a box at the top of a piece of pink paper. Then I wrote: *Your name could be here!* I drew an arrow pointing to the box.

Next I made a circle at the bottom of the paper. I wrote: *Name any picture! I will draw it here.*

Last, I wrote in the middle in great big letters: KAREN'S STATIONERY.

I held it up and looked at it. It needed something. Another word. I knew just the one. I am an excellent speller. But I was not sure how to spell this word. So I looked it up in the dictionary.

Now the page said: KAREN'S EXQUI-SITE STATIONERY.

I held it up again. It *still* was not right. It needed one more thing. Glitter.

I added a glitter border around the page. Now my flier was just right. I was ready to be a door-to-door salesperson. I started with Nannie. *Knock knock.*

"Come in," said Nannie.

I put a big smile on my face and walked into her bedroom.

"Hi!" I said. "I am selling exquisite personal stationery. Would you like to order some?"

I handed Nannie my flier.

"How did you know I needed stationery, Karen? My friend, Sophie, moved to Florida. I have been meaning to write to her for weeks," said Nannie.

"Then this stationery is just what you need!" I said. "How many sheets would you like?"

"Let me see. I have a lot of news to tell Sophie. And I am sure there are other people I have been meaning to write to. I will take ten sheets," said Nannie. "How much will that cost?"

I looked down at my flier. There was no price on it. That was because I did not know how much to charge.

"Um. What would you like to pay?" I asked.

"How about a dollar a page?" said Nannie.

"A dollar? Sold!" I said. That was a lot of money for stationery. "What kind of drawing would you like at the bottom? You can get an extra beautiful drawing for a dollar."

"Surprise me," said Nannie. "I am sure whatever you draw will be beautiful."

Oh, boy! That was simple. I knocked on Daddy's and Elizabeth's door next. I tried my best to sound like the successful salesperson I was.

"Your neighbor, Nannie, ordered ten

22

sheets of this exquisite stationery at a dollar a piece," I said. "How many sheets would you like to order?"

"I am sure we could each use ten sheets," said Elizabeth.

"Sometimes we like to write letters together. How about a dollar and a half to put both our names at the top?" said Daddy.

I was so excited I almost fell down.

"No problem!" I replied. "What kind of drawing would you like at the bottom?"

"I would like stars," said Elizabeth. "All different colors, please."

"I would like red roses," said Daddy. (I was not surprised. Daddy has red roses in his garden.)

I went from room to room. I could hardly believe it. Everyone ordered some of my stationery. (Except for Emily. She is too little.) A dollar a page is a lot of money. So I gave my brothers and sisters a big discount. A good salesperson has to be adaptable.

I went back to my room to count up my orders.

"If I fill all these orders I will have earned plenty of money for my new bike," I told Moosie.

My new Cougar Cat bike. I could see myself riding it now.

Just Like E. T.

In school the next day, I told Hannie and Nancy my news. We were sitting at the back of the room, waiting for Ms. Colman to come in.

"I am getting a new bike!" I said. "A hot pink and purple Cougar Cat."

"That is so cool," said Hannie.

"I will have it just in time for the bike-a-thon," I told them.

"Good morning, class," said Ms. Colman. "Please take your seats. Natalie, will you take attendance?"

Boo. I wish Ms. Colman had picked me. I love to do important jobs for Ms. Colman.

Natalie was very slow. She kept stopping to pull up her socks.

When she finally finished, Ms. Colman said, "I want to tell you a little more about Bike Safety Month and the bike-a-thon. I have some booklets on bike safety from the Motor Vehicles department. Karen, would you please hand them out?"

Yes! I popped up like a jack-in-the-box. I handed out the booklets at top speed. Then I sat down again.

"You do not have to read the booklets now," said Ms. Colman. "Just leaf through them so you can get an idea of the kinds of things you will need to know. You will be expected to know basic traffic rules. And you will need to know the bicyclist's hand signals. They are shown on page ten. Once you have learned these things, you will be given the bike safety test at Town Hall."

Wow. This was serious business. I raised my hand.

"Yes, Karen?" said Ms. Colman.

"What if you do not pass the test? Does the mayor take your bike away?" I asked.

"No one will take your bike away. But you might not be allowed to ride until you pass," replied Ms. Colman. "When you do pass, your name will be printed in the paper."

"I am going to start studying right now," I said.

"We will prepare together. That way each of you should pass the test with no problem," said Ms. Colman.

That was a relief. I did not want to get a brand-new bike and then not be allowed to ride it.

"The other thing you will do at Town Hall is register your bikes. People will be there to help you fill out the forms. Now, about the bike-a-thon. You will need to get sponsors. These are people who will pay you if you reach the finish line. The money they give you will go to the medical center. Pamela, will you please hand out the sponsor sign-up sheets?"

Boo again. Pamela Harding is my best enemy. And Ms. Colman gave *her* the important job.

"Finally, Stoneybrook will hold a bike sale," said Ms. Colman. "It will be held the day of the bike-a-thon. The money that is raised will also be donated to the hospital. If any of you wants to get rid of a second-hand bike, you will need to take it to Town Hall on the day of the sale. I will let you know when that will be. Are there any questions?"

I did not have any questions. I was too busy dreaming about my new bike. I imagined I was riding it in the bike-a-thon. I was pedaling and pedaling. Faster and faster. I took off like an airplane. Up, up, up over the other bikers. My bike was flying through the air. I was just like E. T.

At recess, Nancy said, "I can hardly wait to start signing up sponsors."

"Me, too," I replied. "Also, we will need to get in shape for the bike-a-thon. We have to have a very strict exercise program. I think we should start right now."

I marched over to the monkey bars. Hannie and Nancy were right behind me. We each did three pull-ups. Then we did deep knee bends. We did jumping jacks. We ran around the playground.

Ringg! It was time to go inside. Thank goodness. I was getting tired.

Karen's Announcement

Clink clink! I tapped my glass with my spoon.

"I have a Surprising Announcement to make," I said.

Dinner at the big house was over. I wanted to catch everyone before they left the table.

"We are all ears," said Elizabeth.

"There is going to be a bike-a-thon in a few weeks," I said. "I need sponsors so . . ."

"Wait a minute," said David Michael.

"You are not the only one who needs sponsors. I am going to be in the bike-a-thon, too."

Uh-oh. David Michael and I could not *both* ask everyone to sponsor us. How would they choose? Who would Kristy pick? What about Charlie? And Nannie?

My big-house family was already giving me money for stationery. What if they did not want to give me any more? They would give it all to David Michael. Then what? Daddy must have read my mind.

"I have an idea," he said. "Elizabeth and I will sponsor both of you. Then you can write your names on pieces of paper. The rest of the family will pick your names from a hat. That way you will each have an equal number of sponsors."

This sounded like a very good idea. But wait. There was one problem.

"What about Emily? She cannot sponsor anyone," I said. "What if she picks my name?"

"I will pay for Emily," said Elizabeth.

"All right!" I said. I quickly counted in my head. "That means we each have five sponsors."

Then I remembered I had not called the little house yet. Mommy and Seth would sponsor me for sure.

"Excuse me," I said. "May I use the phone? I want to call Mommy."

Daddy said it would be okay for me to call.

"Hello, Mommy. Guess what? I am going to be in a bike-a-thon. It is to raise money for Stoneybrook Medical Center. Will you sponsor me?"

Mommy said she would. I asked to speak to Seth. I told him my story. He promised to sponsor me, too.

"Um, Seth. Do you think I could call Granny and Grandad? Maybe they would like to be sponsors."

Granny and Grandad are Seth's parents. They live on a farm in Nebraska. I once visited them all by myself.

Seth said he was sure they would like to

hear from me. He gave me their phone number.

"Daddy! May I use the telephone some more?" I asked.

"All right. But just one more call. Other people would like to use the phone, too," Daddy replied.

I dialed the number. Granny answered.

"Hello, Granny!" I said. I asked her how she and Grandad were feeling. Then I told her about the bike-a-thon. She said they would be happy to sponsor me. Yippee!

I had nine sponsors. And I had not even talked to my neighbors yet.

I could see I was very good at making money. Maybe I would become an important banker some day. I would raise lots of money and give it to good causes. I would be front page news. The headline would read:

KAREN BREWER
Most Generous Person in America!

Karen's New Bike

On Saturday morning, I handed Nannie a package wrapped in red gift paper. I had put glitter on the outside. Nannie smiled.

"I think I know what this is," she said. "I hope I am right because I am in the mood to write letters today."

Nannie untied the ribbon and peeked inside. "Oh, Karen! This stationery is beautiful!"

I could tell she meant it. I had tried my best to make the stationery truly exquisite. I had made a few sheets every night. By the time I finished, it looked as pretty as the stationery in stores.

Nannie found her wallet and handed me a new ten-dollar bill.

"Thank you," I said. "It has been a pleasure doing business with you."

I quickly delivered the rest of the orders. Everyone loved their stationery and paid me right away.

I saved Daddy's order for last. I knew I would find him working in his garden.

"Look, Daddy," I said. I held up the stationery. Then I held up all the money I had made. "All this money is for my new bike. And you have not even paid me yet. Can we go downtown today? Please?"

"We sure can," said Daddy. "You have kept your end of our agreement. So I am happy to keep mine."

All right! I asked Kristy to come with me. She knows a lot about bikes. Daddy drove us in the van to the Stoneybrook Bike Shop. I ran straight to the Cougar Cat.

"What do you think of this one?" I asked.

"It is great-looking," said Kristy. "But you need to sit on it to make sure it is comfortable."

I sat on the bike. The seat felt funny. And my knees were too high up, just like when I sat on my old bike.

"Oh, no," I cried. "It is not comfortable. And this is the bike I really, really want."

A salesperson came right over. "Hi, I'm Mike. Let me fix a few things. Then you can try it again."

Mike raised the seat. Then he pointed it a different way. He unscrewed the handle-bars and moved them, too. I sat on the bike again.

"It is perfect," I said. "Thank you!"

"Are you happy with it? Is it the one you want?" asked Daddy.

I stood up and looked at the bike. It was pink and purple, just what I wanted. But then the bike next to it caught my eye. It was a blue and red Cougar Cat. It was pretty, too. Oh, no. Which one? Pink and purple. Blue and red. Pink. Purple. Blue. Red.

Finally I put my hand on the handlebars of the pink and purple bike.

"This is definitely the one I want," I said.

"Good choice," said Kristy. "It is very pretty and it fits you just right."

I sat on my bike while Daddy paid for it.

"All done," he said. "The bike is yours. And this is yours, too."

He handed me a brown paper bag. "Here are two presents," he said. "Mommy asked me to buy them for you."

I opened the bag. Inside were a beautiful new horn and streamers. Mike put them on the bike for me. Then Daddy loaded the bike in the van. As soon as we got home, I made everyone come outside to see it. I rode back and forth in front of the house.

"Cool wheels!" said Charlie.

"Hey, you know what? Now that I have

a new bike, I can donate my old one to the bike sale," I said.

"That is a great idea," said Elizabeth.

"I think I can make the idea even better," said Sam. "I will give your old bike a make-over. That way it will bring in even more money for the hospital."

"Thanks, Sam!" I said. I promised to help him if he needed me.

Then I parked my bike in the garage and hurried inside to call Mommy.

I Love My Bike

After I finished talking with Mommy, I called Nancy.

"I got my new bike!" I said. "Do you want to come over?"

Nancy said she could not wait to see my new bike. She asked her mommy to drive her to the big house.

"I will bring my bike so we can ride together," said Nancy.

"Great. I will call Hannie. I am sure she will want to come, too," I said.

The minute Hannie heard the news, she

said she was going to hang up and come over.

"This bike is awesome!" said Hannie.

"You got streamers, too," said Nancy when she arrived. "Let's go riding!"

We put on our helmets, then started down the street. We were the Three Musketeers on wheels.

"Look everyone, no feet," I said. I pedaled and pedaled. Then I held out my legs and glided down the street. I glided past Callie and Keith. They are four-year-old twins.

"How do you like my new bike?" I said.

They both thought it was very pretty.

Then Linny ran outside, looking for David Michael.

"Notice anything new?" I asked.

"Sure. You got a Cougar. Cool!" said Linny.

Melody and Bill were in their yard. I made them come over to see my bike. They thought it was neat, too.

"Let's have a bike race," said Nancy

when the other kids had left. We lined up across the sidewalk.

"On your mark," said Nancy.

"Get set," said Hannie.

"Go!" I said.

I flew like the wind.

"I won! I won!" I called. I patted my Cougar Cat and tooted the horn.

"I know a game we can play," said Hannie. "David Michael and Linny were playing it yesterday. It looked like fun."

Hannie found a stone and scratched a circle on the sidewalk. Then she made another circle in the center.

"Grab a pebble," she said. "We will take turns riding past the circle and throwing the pebble into the center. The one who gets a bull's-eye wins. But you cannot go slowly. You have to ride by fast."

I thought the game was going to be easy. But the first time I rode by, I missed the circle completely. So did Nancy. Hannie won.

The second time I tried it, I did great.

"Bull's-eye!" I called. I won the game.

"Who wants to ride to the playground?" I asked.

The Stoneybrook Playground is special. That is because the people in Stoneybrook raised money and built it together.

"I want to go," said Hannie.

"Me, too," said Nancy.

"I will be right back," I said. "I have to let my family know where we will be."

I pedaled to the house. It was probably just my imagination, but I seemed to be getting everywhere twice as fast on my new bike. Riding it was so much fun. It was the prettiest bike on the block. I was sure it was the most comfortable. The streamers were definitely the blowiest. The horn was the tootiest.

"I love my bike!" I shouted into the wind.

The Safety Bee

It was Monday morning. I was back at school.

"Everyone, please take your seats," said Ms. Colman. "I would like to go over the bicycle safety booklets with you. I am sure you want to know how to ride safely. And, remember, if you pass the test you will see your name in the newspaper."

Ms. Colman looked in my direction. She knows I love to see my name in the newspaper. (I have been in the newspaper before.)

Ms. Colman wrote some rules on the blackboard:

— *Always wear your helmet*
— *Roll up your pant legs*
— *Follow traffic rules*
— *Ride in single file*
— *No tricks and no passengers*
— *Be sure your bike is safe to ride, with good brakes and tires, a horn or bell, and reflectors*

We talked about each of the rules. Then Ms. Colman said, "You will need to know hand signals, too."

She drew funny stick figures to show us.

Left arm out and down means stop or slow.

Left arm out and bent upward means right turn.

Left arm held straight out means left turn.

45

When we finished practicing the hand signals, Ms. Colman said it was time for our Safety Bee.

This was good news. I am very good at bees. I was even runner-up in the state spelling bee. That is how I got to be in the newspaper one time.

We lined up on one side of the room. Ms. Colman asked us each a question. If we answered it correctly, we continued. If we missed it, we had to sit down. When my turn came, I had a very good question.

"Karen, can you show us the hand signal for a right turn?" asked Ms. Colman.

I stepped out from the line. I put on a make-believe helmet, rolled up make-believe pants, and got on a make-believe bike.

"Okay, now I am turning," I said.

I put my left arm out and bent it upward.

"Very good, Karen," said Ms. Colman. "But will you please try to answer a little more quickly next time?"

46

I promised to try.

The Safety Bee continued. It was not too hard. A lot of kids were still standing when the bell rang for lunch.

After school, Hannie and I decided to ride our bikes so we could practice the safety rules. I even put on pants so I could roll them up. We rode around the block a few times. We followed all the traffic rules. We made sure to signal when we stopped or turned.

We saw lots of little kids along the way. They were riding their tricycles and Big Wheels.

"We should start a bike safety school," I said. "It is never too early to learn how to be safe."

Hannie liked that idea. So we set to work.

Five students came to our school. They were Andrew, Emily, Callie, Keith, and Sari. (Sari is Hannie's sister. She is Emily's age.)

We stayed on the sidewalk and kept away from driveways. We made sure everyone wore a helmet and their pants legs were rolled up.

"First we will show you the hand signals," I said. "Make believe we are playing Simon Says. Do what we do."

We showed them the hand signal for a right turn. No one moved. All they did was look at us.

"What is the matter? Why are you just standing there?" I asked.

"You did not say, 'Simon Says,' " replied Andrew with a big grin on his face.

Hannie and I looked at each other. Teaching little kids is not an easy job.

But bike safety is important. We spent the rest of the afternoon trying.

Taking the Test

We studied bike safety all week at school. We even went on a class trip to the Hall of Safety at a local mall. It was a neat place. I played a video game that let me take a make-believe bike ride. I had to press buttons to signal and stop and everything.

"Eeek!" I called. I was not paying attention and steered my bike down an open manhole. The screen flashed *Game Over! Game Over!* Boo and bullfrogs.

On Thursday Ms. Colman brought in a

chart that showed the parts of a bicycle. We counted twenty-nine parts. Thank goodness we only had to know six of them.

We took a practice test on Friday. I got one answer wrong. I forgot the name of the place where the air goes in the tire.

"That is the air valve," said Ms. Colman.

Finally Saturday came. It was the day of the test at Town Hall. It was the day we would register our bikes, too.

David Michael and I practiced for the test over breakfast.

Then Daddy said, "Are you ready to go, kids?"

We were as ready as we would ever be. Andrew was coming. So were Elizabeth, Nannie, and Emily. At the last minute, Kristy said she could come, too.

"I will cheer you on. And I will get to see how much I know about bikes," she said.

Daddy helped us put our bikes in the van. Then we drove to Town Hall. I had butterflies in my stomach. That is because

I was nervous. What if I did not pass? My name would not appear in the paper. Worse than that, I would not be able to ride my Cougar Cat. That would be awful.

I had to pass the test. I just had to.

Inside Town Hall we saw arrows pointing down to the basement. Lots of kids were already there. I was the first of the Three Musketeers. Hannie and Nancy came in right after me. We stood in line together.

The line was not moving too quickly so we practiced the hand signals while we waited.

"Next in line!" called one of the testers.

"Karen, that is you," said Hannie.

"Good luck," said Nancy.

I walked to the tester's desk and parked my bike. The tester introduced himself. He seemed very nice.

"Hello. My name is Mr. Quinn. If you will just write your name at the top of this sheet, we can get started," he said.

I wrote my name and took a deep breath.

"Here is your first question," said Mr. Quinn. "What is the most important thing to wear when you go bike riding?"

That was easy. "You should always wear a helmet," I said. I decided to show off a little. "And if you are wearing pants, you should roll up the cuffs. That way they will not get caught in your bike and make you have an accident."

"Excellent!" replied Mr. Quinn. I was glad Mr. Quinn was such a friendly tester.

He asked me some more questions. Then he pointed to different parts of my bike and asked me to name them. He pointed to the place on the tire where the air went in. Uh-oh. I was having trouble remembering the name again. I knew it started with V. And it sounded like Valentine. Only it was shorter.

"Valve! Air valve!" I said.

"Excellent!" said Mr. Quinn.

Next he asked me to show him the hand signals. No problem.

The next thing I knew, Mr. Quinn was

saying, "Congratulations. You have passed the bike safety test."

Yippee! David Michael passed, too. So did Hannie and Nancy. Almost all the kids from Ms. Colman's class passed.

We got green badges that said, "Ride Safely, Have Fun." We were told to watch for our names in the paper. Next stop, bike registration.

Important Numbers

*T*ap, *tap, tap. Tap, tap, tap.* I was tapping my foot. That is because I was gigundoly bored. The line for bike registering was very long. It was taking forever. And the Three Musketeers were on different lines, since our last names do not begin with the same letter. *Tap, tap, tap. Tap, tap, tap.*

"Next in line!" called a voice.

I stepped up to the town official. Her name tag said *Brenda Miller.*

"Please bring your bike to the white line," she said. "I will inspect it for safety.

Then I will copy down the manufacturer's registration number."

"It is very safe," I said. "I just got it. It is beautiful, isn't it?"

Some people are friendlier than others. Ms. Miller was not as friendly as Mr. Quinn. I was waiting for her to tell me my bike was excellent. But she did not.

She checked the brakes, squeezed the tires, and copied the manufacturer's registration number onto a form.

"The manufacturer's number is stamped right here on this bar," said Ms. Miller. "It is an important number to know in case you ever need to identify your bike."

"Thank you," I replied.

My number was six-three-four-two. I liked it.

Next Ms. Miller wrote down the name of my bike. Cougar Cat. And the colors. Pink and purple. She wrote down how long I had owned it. One week. She asked for the exact spelling of my name, my date of birth, my address, and my phone number. She wrote another number on the top of the form and copied it onto a yellow sticker. She handed the sticker to me.

"Your registration number is two-eight-nine-two. Use that number if you ever have a question about your registration," Ms. Miller said. "Next!"

"Is that it? Am I registered?" I asked.

"That is it," said Ms. Miller. "Next!"

I did it. I had registered my bike at Town Hall. I felt very grown-up.

When I got back to the big house, I checked on Sam. He was in the backyard working on my old bike.

"It does not look so old anymore," I said.

The spoke on the back wheel was fixed. And a fresh coat of white paint was on it.

"Are you going to leave it white?" I asked.

"No. This is the undercoat," said Sam. "What color would you like it to be?"

"I think red would be nice. With white trim," I said.

"Consider it done," replied Sam.

After lunch I called Hannie, then Nancy. We talked about the test and about registering our bikes.

Then we made a plan for Sunday. We were going to pack a picnic lunch and ride our bikes to the playground again.

"We are officially registered bike riders in the town of Stoneybrook," I said to Hannie. "This will be our celebration picnic."

Missing!

Hannie and Nancy arrived at the big house at eleven o'clock sharp on Sunday. It was a beautiful day for a picnic.

Nannie helped me make sandwiches. Hannie brought fruit and juice. Nancy brought dessert.

"You have quite a feast here," said Nannie. "Have a very good time. And remember to ride safely."

We put on our helmets. We rolled up the cuffs of our pants. Then we walked our bikes down the driveway, looked both ways, and rode to the playground.

The bike racks were pretty full. We found three spots near each other and locked up our bikes. Then we looked for a place to set up our picnic.

"Are we hungry yet?" I asked.

None of us was hungry. So we played awhile. First we rode on the swings. Then we jumped rope. Then we took turns on the seesaw.

"Is anyone hungry now?" asked Hannie.

By then we were all hungry. It was time for our picnic. We sat down on our blanket and filled our plastic cups with apple juice. I lifted mine up the way grown-ups do when they want to say something important.

"Happy bike registration!" I said.

"To our bikes!" said Nancy.

"To the Three Musketeers!" said Hannie. "Long may we ride."

We tapped our cups together and drank our apple juice.

The picnic was lots of fun. We thought about the places we would ride our bikes to together. When we finished eating we played some more. We joined a game of freeze tag. Then we played spud. Then we rode on the swings again. It was the best day.

"I have to go home soon," said Nancy. "I promised not to be back too late."

We packed up our picnic things, then went back to our bikes. Hannie's bike was there. Nancy's bike was there.

"Does anyone see my bike?" I asked.

My stomach was doing flip-flops. My bike was not where I thought I had left it. Maybe I was just looking in the wrong place.

"It was right here," said Nancy. "It was next to ours."

We looked up and down the rack. My bike was not there. I was sure I had locked it up. But the lock I had used was old and rusty and not very strong. Now my brand-new Cougar Cat was missing.

"Someone must have stolen it," said Nancy.

"Maybe someone just took it for a ride and brought it back to the playground," I said. "Come look with me."

We looked and looked. But we could not find my bike. I burst into tears.

Nancy put her arm around me. "Come on," she said. "We will walk home together."

"You have to call the police right away," said Hannie.

Hannie and Nancy walked their bikes home with me. I wished one of them could have given me a ride. It would have been faster. But taking passengers is against the rules. The walk home seemed to last forever.

I found Daddy working in the garden. The minute I saw him, I burst into tears again. He jumped up and ran to me.

"Karen, honey, what happened?" he asked.

I told Daddy the whole sad story.

The Police

"We will go right to the police station to report your missing bike," said Daddy. "We will bring a copy of your bike registration form with us."

I said good-bye to Hannie and Nancy. (Nancy was going to Hannie's house to wait for her mommy to pick her up.) Then Daddy and I drove to the police station.

Officer Benitez was on duty. She helped me once before when I turned in a wallet I had found on the street.

"Hi, Officer Benitez," I said. "Remember me?"

"Yes, I do. Your name is Karen," she replied. "How can I help you today?"

"Well, this time I did not find something. I lost something," I said. "I lost my brand-new Cougar Cat bike. I guess it was stolen."

"We have the bike registration papers here," said Daddy.

"I am sorry to hear about your bike," said Officer Benitez. "There has been a rash of stolen bicycles. It is very good that you have the registration form. It will make your bike easy to identify if any of the stolen bikes turns up."

Officer Benitez left to make a copy of the registration form. When she came back, she said, "We will be looking into this problem. I promise to keep you informed about our investigation."

We thanked Officer Benitez. I knew she would keep her promise and call if my bike

was found. But I did not really expect to hear from her. I was sure the police had more important things to do than look for my stolen Cougar Cat.

On the way back to the big house I saw kids riding around on their bikes. I missed mine. I wished I could go back to bed and start the day over. I would watch my bike every second to make sure it did not get stolen.

When I got home I called Mommy and Seth to tell them what happened. They were both very sorry. Mommy said I should try my best to be patient. She said the police might find my bike after all. But I did not think so.

The next thing I did was plop down in the TV room. I did not even turn on the TV. I just sat and moped. Kristy and Sam tried to keep me company.

"I am really sorry about your bike," said Kristy. "It was brand new and I know how much you loved it."

"I miss it," I said. "But that is not the

only bad thing. I was supposed to ride it in the bike-a-thon. I signed up a lot of sponsors. How am I supposed to ride in it now?"

"You do not have to worry about that," said Sam. "I promise to have your old bike ready in time. It is almost ready now. I discovered a small problem with the brakes. But I will have them working like new very soon."

"Thank you," I said.

The news made me feel only a little better. At least I could ride in the bike-a-thon. But I would not be riding my great new bike. Boo.

Detectives

On Monday I told everyone at school about my missing bike. They all felt gigundoly sorry for me. Even Pamela, my best enemy, said she felt bad.

By the end of the day, I had thought of a plan. I told Hannie about it on the way home from school.

"The police are very busy with other important cases. If I am going to get my bike back there have to be more detectives looking for it. Will you help me find my bike?" I asked.

"Sure," said Hannie. "I can start this afternoon."

Hannie went home to drop off her books and change her clothes. She came over to the big house with her bike and helmet. By then I had asked David Michael to help.

"I asked Linny, too," said Hannie. "But he is going to play softball with some other kids."

"There must be someone else who wants to be an important detective," I said.

We saw Callie and Keith. They were too little.

I saw Melody and Bill Korman. They had already promised Linny they would play softball.

Then Timmy and Scott Hsu came running toward us.

"I hear you are looking for detectives," said Timmy. "My bike was stolen yesterday. You can count me in."

"You can count me in, too. Maybe we will find both bikes," said Scott.

That made five detectives. It was a good team.

"We are looking for a pink and purple Cougar Cat bike," I said to Timmy and Scott.

"I know," said Timmy. "I saw you riding it over the weekend. My bike is a blue and green Ross."

"Okay, team. We should meet again here at five o'clock sharp," I said. "I hope we will have found our bikes by then. This is an important mission. Good luck."

Scott and Timmy were going to investigate on foot. David Michael decided to go with them. I wanted to stick with Hannie. She was going to ride her bike. I knew we could cover more ground if we rode.

"Maybe Maria will lend me her bike," I said. "I will ask her."

Maria Kilbourne lives next door to Hannie. She could not investigate with us. But she was happy to lend me her bike. I walked it home and found my helmet. I also found a magnifying glass in the play-room. I could use it to search for clues.

"I am ready," I said. "Keep your eyes open for tire tracks and other suspicious clues."

There was nothing suspicious on our street. So we rode up and down the next street. And the next. We were halfway down the third street when I noticed something.

"Psst! Look. I see tire tracks over there," I said.

I pulled out my magnifying glass. I did not want to risk losing the tracks. We followed them up the street and into a yard.

At the end of the tracks was a bike. But it was not my bike. This one was black and silver. It was propped against a tree. A boy was leaning against the tree reading a book.

"Hi," he said.

"Hi," I replied. "We are looking for a couple of missing bikes. Have you seen any lately?"

I described the bikes. The boy had not seen them.

"Thanks, anyway," I said.

We went back to the street. I stopped to poke through a garbage can. Yuck. It was a dirty job. But someone had to do it.

"What are you looking for? I do not think a bike could fit in there," said Hannie.

"I know that," I replied. "Maybe I will find my streamers or my horn. At least I would know my bike had been here."

I did not find any clues in the garbage can.

It was almost five o'clock so we went back to our meeting place. No one had any leads. We planned to try again the next day after school.

You Are Under Arrest

The next afternoon I borrowed Maria's bike again, and Timmy borrowed Bill Korman's. We borrowed locks, too. We did not want any more bikes to be stolen.

"We should go to the playground," I said to my fellow detectives. "That was the scene of the crime. There are bound to be clues or suspicious characters lurking around there."

Everyone agreed that this was a good plan. We rode to the playground in single file. We made sure to follow the traffic rules and to signal whenever we had to.

When we got there we locked our bikes in the bike rack.

"Meet back here in twenty minutes," I said.

We marched into the playground together. Then each of us went in a different direction to investigate.

Some kids were sitting on a bench eating ice cream and talking. I sat down near them. I thought they might be talking about where they stashed the bikes. They were not. They were talking about a birthday party they had been to.

Then I saw a very suspicious thing. Something bright yellow was hanging out of the pocket of a boy on a swing. From where I was sitting, it looked like one of my streamers. I moved closer to get a better look. It was not a streamer. It was the boy's handkerchief. I hoped the other detectives were having better luck than I was.

The next thing I knew a girl was riding by the playground on a bike. A pink and purple bike. It looked like *my* pink and purple bike.

"Stop in the name of the law!" I called.

I ran out of the playground and caught up to her.

"You are under arrest," I said. "Take your feet off the pedals and put your hands in the air!"

"I cannot do that," said the girl. "I will fall off my bike if I do."

"You mean you will fall off *my* bike," I said. "That is my bike and I want it back right now."

"I do not know why you think this is your bike. I got it for my birthday last week," said the girl.

"Prove it," I said.

The girl showed me a license plate on the back. Her name was on it. Her name was Susan.

"Well, Susan," I said. "You could have stolen my bike and then put your name plate on."

"I could have. But I did not," Susan replied.

I remembered what Ms. Miller said when I registered my bike. She said I might need the manufacturer's registration number to identify my bike some day. I asked if I could look for the number.

"Go ahead. See for yourself," said Susan. "This is not your bike."

I looked on the bar for a number. I found one. Oops. It was not my number. My number was six-three-four-two. This number was nine-three-three-one.

"Sorry," I said. "It really looks just like my bike. My bike was stolen on Sunday."

"I am sorry your bike was stolen. But you should be more careful the next time you try arresting someone," said Susan.

She rode away on her bike. It really did look just like mine.

I was a very embarrassed detective.

Found!

I decided to search for my bike again on Wednesday. I was rounding up my detectives when I ran into Bill Korman.

"Are you looking for more detectives? *My* bike was just stolen, too," he said.

"Come on," I said. "We are going on a bike hunt right now."

Then Melody Korman said she wanted to come. And Maria Kilbourne. And Linny. That made nine detectives. If this top-notch team could not succeed, no one could.

We were able to borrow enough bikes for everyone to ride. This time we broke up into groups of two or three. My partner was Bill. This was good. Bill is a little older than I am. So he is allowed to ride farther from home than I can by myself.

"Follow me," said Bill.

"I will be right behind you all the way," I replied.

We rode up one street and down another. Up one, down another. Soon we were in a neighborhood I did not know. It looked a little run-down.

There were bikes all over the place, some with riders, some parked in driveways. Most of them were old. But I saw a few new ones, too. In fact, I saw a girl riding down the street on a new bike that looked just like mine.

I had found my bike. I was absolutely, totally, positively, one hundred percent sure. (I think.)

My stomach started doing flip-flops. I wanted to chase the girl. But after yesterday, I thought this might not be such a good idea.

"Bill, wait up!" I said. "I see my bike!"

Bill signaled that he was going to stop. Then he pulled his bike onto the sidewalk.

"It is over there," I said.

The girl had just parked the bike in the driveway of a run-down house.

"It sure does look like your bike," said Bill. "We will have to investigate."

"We better be careful. The people who live there might not like us snooping around their house," I said.

"Do not worry. I will check it out. But how will we know if it is really your bike?" asked Bill.

"The manufacturer's registration number should be on the cross bar," I said. "The number is six-three-four-two."

"You stay here and keep an eye on the house. If anyone comes out, blow the horn to let me know. I will check the registration number," said Bill.

Bill crept up the driveway. I kept my eye on the house to make sure no one came out.

Then Bill came running back.

"It is your bike," he said. "We found it!"

"We have to go home and report this right away!" I said.

We memorized the address so we could tell the police. Then we jumped on our bikes and raced home.

I was extra excited. We had found my bike. Thank goodness it looked okay. I could hardly wait to ride it again.

Hooray!

Bill and I reached the big house just as Daddy was getting home from a meeting.

"Daddy! Daddy!" I called. "Guess what! We found my bike."

I told him the story. He went straight inside to call Officer Benitez. She took down the information and promised to call us back.

That night we were having Nannie's excellent homemade lasagna with salad for dinner. But I could hardly eat a bite. I was too busy listening for the phone to ring.

Finally it did! I raced to answer it. It was for Kristy.

"Why hasn't Officer Benitez called back?" I asked Daddy.

"You must be patient, Karen. The police might not call us until tomorrow," Daddy replied.

"Tomorrow! I do not think I can wait that long," I said.

"I think you can," said Daddy.

Daddy was right. I made it through the night and the next day at school. When I got home, Nannie said the police *still* had not called.

"Maybe we should call Officer Benitez again to remind her," I said.

"I am sure she has not forgotten," replied Nannie.

That meant I could not call. Boo. I wandered outside and sat on the curb. I could hear the phone from there if it rang.

I had not been sitting there very long

when something gigundoly exciting happened. A police car pulled up to my house.

Officer Benitez and another officer got out. His badge said *Officer Myers*. The two police officers had big smiles on their faces. In a minute I knew why.

Officer Myers proudly lifted my bike from the back of the car and set it down in front of me.

"Hooray! Yippee! Hooray!" I shouted.

Nannie ran outside with Emily and Andrew behind her. They found me hugging my bike as if it were a person.

Then I remembered my manners.

"Thank you for bringing my bike back," I said to the officers.

"You are a good detective, Karen," said Officer Benitez. "The bike was in the driveway just as you reported it."

"What will happen to the girl who took it?" asked Nannie.

"It turns out the girl did not steal Karen's bike," said Officer Benitez. "Her parents

wanted to buy her a bicycle. They could not afford a new one, so they watched for ads for second-hand bikes. One day they saw a flier posted in the grocery store. When they called the number they were thrilled to have found an almost new, expensive bike that would cost much less money than it would in a store. So they bought it. Now they understand that it was so cheap because it was stolen."

"If the girl did not take it, who did?" I asked.

"We do not know that yet. Luckily the girl's parents held onto the phone number they called in case there were any problems with the bike. We have the number and will be following up," said Officer Benitez.

"The number may provide clues to finding the other missing bikes," said Officer Myers. "Right now we are just happy you have your bike back safe and sound."

"Me, too!" I said.

I could not decide what to do next.

Should I take my bike for a ride? Or should I call everyone to tell them the good news?

I was not ready to leave my bike yet. And I wanted to tell everyone right away. So I carried my bike inside and sat on it while I called my friends and Mommy.

Good News

That night I started thinking about the girl I had seen riding my bike. I felt bad for her. She did not have a bike to ride anymore. I knew her family did not have enough money to buy her a new one. Hmm. I decided to find Sam.

"How are you doing with my old bike?" I asked.

"Come take a look. It is almost ready for the bike sale," replied Sam. "I just need to test the brakes a couple more times to make sure they are safe. We cannot take any chances when it comes to brakes."

Sam led me out to the garage. At first I did not see the bike. Then Sam proudly pulled up the sheet that was covering it and said, "Ta-da!"

The bike looked great. It was shiny red with white trim. It would be perfect for the girl to ride. I told Sam my idea.

"Instead of giving the bike to the bike sale, maybe we could give it to the girl who had to return my new bike," I said. "She is smaller than I am so this bike would fit her fine. And you made it look really beautiful."

"That is a terrific idea, Karen," said Sam. "I will have it ready for you tomorrow afternoon."

I checked out my plan with Daddy. He liked it, too.

On Friday afternoon, Sam said, "The bike is ready to go."

"Thanks," I said. "It needs just one more thing."

I ran upstairs and found some red ribbon.

I made two big bows and tied them onto the handlebars. Now the bike was ready.

Charlie offered to help. He loaded the bike into the van and the three of us drove to the girl's house.

I walked to the front door and rang the bell. A woman answered it. The girl was standing next to her.

"Hi," I said. "I am Karen Brewer. The bike you had belonged to me."

Suddenly the girl and her mother looked worried.

"Oh, I know you bought my bike and did not steal it," I said. "So it is not fair that you do not have a bike to ride now. Would you like to have this one?"

Sam was wheeling my old bicycle up the path. As soon as the girl saw it she started to smile.

"It is beautiful," she said. She turned to her mother. "May I keep it?"

"Just a minute, Polly," said her mother. "Could you please tell me how much this bike costs," she said to me.

"It does not cost anything," I replied. "It is a present. To say thank you for taking good care of my other bike while you had it."

The girl looked at her mother. I could see how much she wanted to keep the bike. Her mother had to think for a minute. Then she said, "Thank you for this gift, Karen. You are very thoughtful."

"Now I can be in the bike-a-thon!" said Polly.

"Great," I said. "I am going to be in the bike-a-thon, too. I will see you there."

We waved good-bye. I got into the van with Sam and Charlie. Charlie stopped at a store downtown on the way home.

"We want to buy you a really good lock for your new bike," he said. "Then it will not be so easy to steal."

"Thank you," I replied. I would feel better leaving my bike with a brand-new lock on it.

The next day was Saturday. The phone rang early. It was Officer Myers.

"I have good news," he said. "The phone

number led us to a stash of stolen bikes that were about to be sold. We are having the bikes identified now. Your friends, Timmy Hsu and Bill Korman, already have their bikes back. And the thieves are under arrest."

More good news! Now we could all be in the bike-a-thon. It was only two weeks away.

The Bike-a-thon

"I have so many sponsors I can hardly believe it," I said. "If I finish the course, I will get a lot of money to give to the hospital."

I was standing outside Town Hall with Hannie and Nancy. We were in line waiting to hand in our sign-up sheets so we could enter the bike-a-thon.

David Michael and Linny were ahead of us. Bill, Melody, Timmy, and Scott were behind us. Then I saw a girl walking by with a red bike that looked very familiar. It was Polly.

"Hi, Polly!" I called. I introduced her to Hannie and Nancy. We talked for awhile. Then she joined some kids from her class.

School had let out for the summer. But most of the kids from our class were at the bike-a-thon. Even Ms. Colman was there. She was going to ride, too.

"Hi, Ms. Colman!" I called.

"Next!" said a voice. It was Mr. Quinn.

"Hi, Mr. Quinn," I said. "I have a lot of sponsors."

"Excellent!" replied Mr. Quinn. He stamped my sign-up sheet and gave me my number. I was number eighty-one in the bike-a-thon. I pinned the number on my shirt.

I waited for Hannie and Nancy.

"Let's try to ride together all the way," I said. "But if we get separated, we can meet at the finish line."

We strapped on our helmets. Then we hopped on our bikes and started pedaling.

We rode on a long, winding course

around Stoneybrook. The streets were closed to traffic. Cups of juice were set up on tables along the way in case anyone got thirsty. Music from the school band was piped in over a loudspeaker to keep up everyone's spirits.

We pedaled and pedaled. And pedaled and pedaled. Once I thought I might have to get off and walk my bike. We were going up a very steep hill. My knees were starting to ache.

I am not going to stop. I am not going to stop, I told myself.

I started to feel like *The Little Engine That Could*. And you know what? I made it up the hill!

When I reached the top I realized I had lost Hannie and Nancy. I would just have to meet them later.

I saw a table with juice at the top of the hill. I grabbed a cup, then kept on going. I rode and rode until I could see the finish line. Then I pedaled as fast as I could.

"I am coming through!" I called. With my streamers flying in the breeze, I crossed the finish line.

"I did it! I did it!" I cried.

Both my families were there waiting for me. They were jumping up and down and cheering.

"Way to go!" I heard Kristy call.

I proudly handed in my number eighty-one and got a free ice pop. It was cold and delicious.

I ran back to the finish line to find Hannie and Nancy and join my families.

The bike-a-thon was over by early afternoon. The bike sale was over, too. It had been going on at the same time.

Mrs. Titus, our school principal, asked us to be patient while the pledges were added up. Finally she announced how much money we had earned for the hospital and introduced Mr. Finney, the hospital director.

"Thanks to you and to lots of others who helped out, the Stoneybrook Medical Cen-

ter will be able to build a much needed new wing," said Mr. Finney. "The bike-a-thon was a great success. You should be very proud of what you have done today."

I patted my new bike. I did feel proud.

It was time to say good-bye to my friends. But I knew I would be seeing them soon. We had a lot of bike riding to look forward to.

About the Author

ANN M. MARTIN lives in New York City and loves animals, especially cats. She has two cats of her own, Mouse and Rosie.

Other books by Ann M. Martin that you might enjoy are *Stage Fright*; *Me and Katie (the Pest)*; and the books in *The Baby-sitters Club* series.

Ann likes ice cream and *I Love Lucy*. And she has her own little sister, whose name is Jane.

Little Sister

Don't miss #63

KAREN'S MOVIE

"That sounds great," said Kristy. "Sam could probably help you make the movie. He knows a little about filmmaking."

"I will be right back," I said to Kristy. "I want to call Hannie and Nancy to tell them my idea. Maybe they will help me with the movie."

I called Nancy first.

"Guess what!" I said. "I am going to make a movie for my granny and grandad. Do you want to help?"

Nancy was really excited. She said she would come over right away. I called Hannie next. She was excited, too. Her mom said she would drive her to my house.

I was gigundoly happy. I wanted my friends with me on this important day. I was about to begin my movie career.

If you like the **Baby-sitters Little Sister** books you'll love **The Kids in Ms. Colman's Class**!

A new series by Ann M. Martin

Don't miss #1
Teacher's Pet

Nancy looked down the hallway. She knew where her room was. She walked toward it very slowly. Natalie ran by her. Omar ran by her. Ricky ran by her.

"Hey, slowpoke!" Ricky called to Nancy.

Nancy stopped outside Ms. Colman's room. She poked her head in the door.

"BOO!" shouted Bully Bobby.

"Aughh!" shrieked Nancy.

"Scared you, you baby," said Bobby. He glared at Nancy.

Nancy took another step into the room. She saw Natalie, Ricky, the Barkan twins, and some other kids she knew from kindergarten and first grade. And she saw a lot of kids she did not know.

"Good morning, boys and girls," said a grown-up's voice.

Standing in the doorway behind Nancy was Ms. Colman. She was smiling. She was smiling even though Ian Johnson was pretending to brush his hair with an eraser. And even though Audrey Green was giving herself a tattoo with a red Magic Marker. And even though Hank Reubens was tickling Leslie Morris and had made Leslie fall on the floor.

Nancy looked at Hannie. She was about to lean over and whisper, "Psst! Hey! Hannie Papadakis!"

But Hannie was busy whispering to Sara Ford who sat in front of her. Then Terri Barkan turned around and asked Hannie if she could borrow a pencil. And then Ricky passed a note to Hannie.

Nancy sighed. She gazed around the room. Who would be her second-grade best friend?

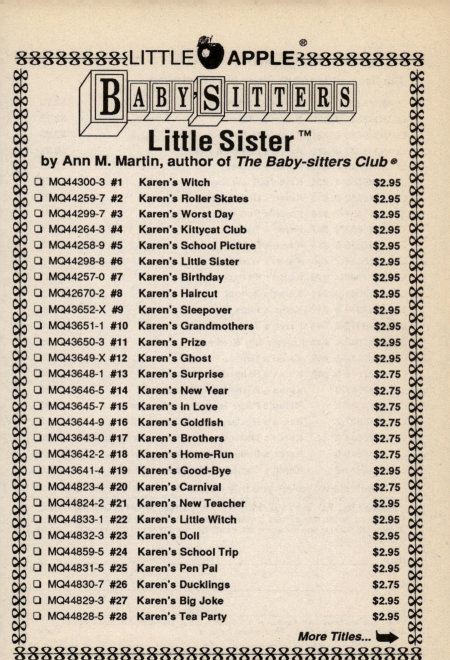

LITTLE APPLE®

BABY-SITTERS Little Sister™

by Ann M. Martin, author of *The Baby-sitters Club*®

❏	MQ44300-3	#1	Karen's Witch	$2.95
❏	MQ44259-7	#2	Karen's Roller Skates	$2.95
❏	MQ44299-7	#3	Karen's Worst Day	$2.95
❏	MQ44264-3	#4	Karen's Kittycat Club	$2.95
❏	MQ44258-9	#5	Karen's School Picture	$2.95
❏	MQ44298-8	#6	Karen's Little Sister	$2.95
❏	MQ44257-0	#7	Karen's Birthday	$2.95
❏	MQ42670-2	#8	Karen's Haircut	$2.95
❏	MQ43652-X	#9	Karen's Sleepover	$2.95
❏	MQ43651-1	#10	Karen's Grandmothers	$2.95
❏	MQ43650-3	#11	Karen's Prize	$2.95
❏	MQ43649-X	#12	Karen's Ghost	$2.95
❏	MQ43648-1	#13	Karen's Surprise	$2.75
❏	MQ43646-5	#14	Karen's New Year	$2.75
❏	MQ43645-7	#15	Karen's in Love	$2.75
❏	MQ43644-9	#16	Karen's Goldfish	$2.75
❏	MQ43643-0	#17	Karen's Brothers	$2.75
❏	MQ43642-2	#18	Karen's Home-Run	$2.75
❏	MQ43641-4	#19	Karen's Good-Bye	$2.95
❏	MQ44823-4	#20	Karen's Carnival	$2.75
❏	MQ44824-2	#21	Karen's New Teacher	$2.95
❏	MQ44833-1	#22	Karen's Little Witch	$2.95
❏	MQ44832-3	#23	Karen's Doll	$2.95
❏	MQ44859-5	#24	Karen's School Trip	$2.95
❏	MQ44831-5	#25	Karen's Pen Pal	$2.95
❏	MQ44830-7	#26	Karen's Ducklings	$2.75
❏	MQ44829-3	#27	Karen's Big Joke	$2.95
❏	MQ44828-5	#28	Karen's Tea Party	$2.95

More Titles... ➡

Available wherever you buy books, or use this order form.

- -

Scholastic Inc., P.O. Box 7502, 2931 E. McCarty Street, Jefferson City, MO 65102

Please send me the books I have checked above. I am enclosing $ _____
(please add $2.00 to cover shipping and handling). Send check or money order - no cash
or C.O.Ds please.

Name _____ Birthdate _____

Address _____

City _____ State/Zip _____

Please allow four to six weeks for delivery. Offer good in U.S.A. only. Sorry, mail orders are not
available to residents to Canada. Prices subject to change.   BLS793

Karen Brewer and her friends are jumping for joy!

All-new!

Baby-Sitters
Little Sister®

Comes with a colorful jump rope!

Jump Rope Rhymes Pack

You'll love singing and jumping along with the rhymes, games, and lots more inside this new Little Sister pack! Learn all the alphabet rhymes, classic rhymes and Double Dutch rhymes from the book—then practice your fancy footwork with the jump rope that's included. It's easy to have a ton of fun with your friends, just like Karen does!

Coming in July.

BS2SJ1194

Meet some new friends in a brand-new
series just right for <u>you</u>.
Starring **Baby-sitters Little Sister**
Karen Brewer...
and everyone else in the second grade.

Look for THE KIDS IN MS. COLMAN'S CLASS #1: TEACHER'S PET.
Coming to your bookstore in September.

MC 195